Other books by Marcus Pfister

THE RAINBOW FISH*
THE CHRISTMAS STAR*
DAZZLE THE DINOSAUR*
PENGUIN PETE
PENGUIN PETE'S NEW FRIENDS
PENGUIN PETE AND PAT
PENGUIN PETE, AHOY!
PENGUIN PETE AND LITTLE TIM
HOPPER
HOPPER HUNTS FOR SPRING
HOPPER'S EASTER SURPRISE
HANG ON, HOPPER!
CHRIS & CROC

** also available in Spanish*

Published in the United States, Great Britain, Canada, Australia, and New Zealand in 1988 by North-South Books, an imprint of Nord-Süd Verlag, AG.
First paperback edition published in 1995.

Distributed in the United States by North-South Books, Inc., New York

Library of Congress Catalog Card Number: 87-32203

British Library Cataloguing in Publication Data
Siegenthaler, Kathrin
Santa Claus and the Woodcutter.
I. Title II. Pfister, Marcus
III. Wie Sankt Nikolaus einen Gehiffen fand. *English*
833'.914[J] PZ7

ISBN 1-55858-027-1 (trade binding)
3 5 7 9 11 TB 10 8 6 4 2
ISBN 1-55858-505-2 (paperback)
1 3 5 7 9 PB 10 8 6 4 2

Printed in Italy

Kathrin Siegenthaler

Santa Claus

and the Woodcutter

Translated by Elizabeth D. Crawford

Illustrated by Marcus Pfister

North-South Books
New York

It was December, and winter had covered the countryside with a thick blanket of snow. The little house at the edge of the forest seemed even more forlorn and cut off from the world than usual.

For many years the woodcutter had lived in this little cottage all alone.

He had not been into the village for a long time – he didn't really like to go there at all. The people often whispered behind his back about the strange man from the woods. And the children made fun of his patched coat.

All the same, his sled was packed full of wood again now, so the woodcutter set off for the village.

But this time the village people had no time to bother about him. They were busy with last-minute preparations for the visit from Santa Claus. The houses were beautifully decorated, and the children could hardly wait until evening.

The woodcutter had completely forgotten. Of course! Today was Christmas Eve! After he sold his wood, he made his way home a little sadly. It had been a long time since Santa Claus had come to see him.

That same afternoon the woodcutter was again sitting in his cottage. Suddenly he heard a soft tinkling of bells coming from the path through the woods. He ran to the window and, yes – it really was! Santa Claus was driving toward the village with his little donkey and heavily laden sleigh.

The woodcutter opened the door and called, "Greetings, Santa Claus! Wouldn't you like to come in and have a cup of hot tea with me?"

Santa Claus gladly accepted his friendly invitation. They drank a cup of tea together, and Santa Claus had a chance to warm himself by the stove. At last it began to get dark, and Santa Claus said, "You have my heartfelt thanks, my friend. Now I must go on if I'm to get to the children in time."

Soon Santa Claus disappeared into a swirl of snow. The woodcutter had to go out into the snowstorm, too; he needed some more wood for his stove. So he plodded out onto the forest path, and what did he see there? Everywhere lay nuts, oranges, gingerbread men, and small presents. The path was covered with them. Did Santa Claus leave all this for him?

In the meantime, Santa Claus had nearly reached the village. Going downhill he sat comfortably in the sleigh. Going uphill he helped the little donkey pull the heavy load. The journey had been long and hard, but he was nearly at the end. Santa Claus was already happily picturing the beaming faces of the children.

7

But when he got out of his sleigh at the edge of the village to unload the sack, he couldn't believe his eyes. The huge sack was empty – totally, utterly empty! Very quickly Santa Claus discovered a hole in the sack. During the bumpy journey it had become larger and larger, and so finally all the nuts, fruit, and packages had rolled out into the snow.

What was he going to do now? It was too late to make the long trip back. The snow that had fallen in the meantime was sure to have covered everything up. Must he now go to the children empty-handed? Santa Claus sank down on the edge of his sleigh in despair.

Suddenly he saw a figure appear on the horizon, tiny at first, then larger and larger and more distinct. Who would want to be out and about so late in this deep snow? It was a man, carrying a gigantic sack on his back. He seemed very excited. From far off Santa Claus heard him calling, “Santa Claus! Wait! Wait for me!”

When the man came closer, Santa Claus recognized the friendly woodcutter who had invited him in. He had followed Santa Claus and had collected everything and packed it into a sack.

Santa Claus hugged him. "How can I ever thank you?" he asked. "I never did ask you your name, by the way."

"My first name is Rupert, and that's what they call me in the village."

"I've been looking for a helper like you for a long, long time, Rupert. Would you like to visit the children with me?"

Would Rupert like to! His eyes sparkled with joy.

So together they both knocked on the door of the first house. How astonished the grown-ups and the children were that Santa Claus had Rupert, of all people, with him! But when Santa Claus told the story of the lost presents, they were all ashamed that they had always treated Rupert so badly. And one woman even gave him a warm new winter coat.

From that day on Rupert was Santa Claus's faithful helper. Every year at the end of December you can see them both driving through the snowy woods to the village, where the children are always happily waiting for them.